EARLY BIRD
STORIES

Tug! Tug!
&
Lots of Spots

Early ★ Reader

First American edition published in 2020 by Lerner Publishing Group, Inc.

An original concept by Jenny Jinks
Copyright © 2020 Jenny Jinks

Illustrated by Daniela Dogliani

First published by Maverick Arts Publishing Limited

Maverick
arts publishing

Licensed Edition
Tug! Tug! & Lots of Spots

Lerner Publications Company
An imprint of Lerner Publishing Group, Inc.
241 First Avenue North
Minneapolis, MN 55401 USA

For reading levels and more information, look up this title at
www.lernerbooks.com.

Main body text set in Mikado. Typeface provided by HVD Fonts.

Library of Congress Cataloging-in-Publication Data

Names: Jinks, Jenny, author. | Dogliani, Daniela, illustrator. | Jinks, Jenny. Tug! Tug! | Jinks, Jenny. Lots of spots.
Title: Tug! Tug! ; & Lots of spots / by Jenny Jinks ; illustrated by Daniela Dogliani.
Description: Minneapolis : Lerner Publications, [2020] | Series: Early bird readers. Pink (Early bird stories) | "An original concept by Jenny Jinks." | Originally published in Horsham, West Sussex by Maverick Arts Publishing Ltd in 2018.
Identifiers: LCCN 2019008644 | ISBN 9781541578050 (lb : alk. paper) | ISBN 978-1-5415-8284-2 (EB pdf) | ISBN 978-1-5415-7805-0 (lib. bdg.) | ISBN 978-1-5415-8728-1 (pb : alk. paper)
Subjects: LCSH: Readers (Primary)
Classification: LCC PE1119 .J564 2020 | DDC 428.6/2—dc23

LC record available at https://lccn.loc.gov/2019008644

Manufactured in the United States of America
1-46882-47786-4/26/2019

EARLY BIRD STORIES™

Tug! Tug!
&
Lots of Spots

Jenny Jinks

Illustrated by
Daniela Dogliani

Lerner Publications ◆ Minneapolis

The Letter "Y"

Trace the lowercase and uppercase letter with a finger. Sound out the letter.

*Down,
around,
up,
down,
around*

*Down,
lift,
down,
down*

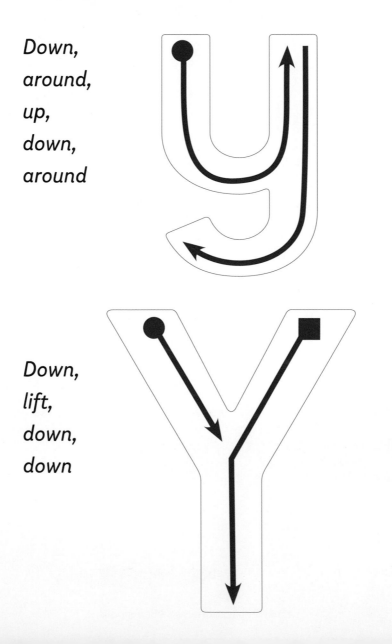

Some words to familiarize:

carrot   tug   Flop

High-frequency words:

has a the it and

Tips for Reading *Tug! Tug!*

- Practice the words listed above before reading the story.

- If the reader struggles with any of the other words, ask them to look for sounds they know in the word. Encourage them to sound out the words and help them read the words if necessary.

- After reading the story, ask the reader who gets the carrot in the end.

Fun Activity

Discuss what other animals might like to eat carrots.

Tug! Tug!

Ben has a carrot.

Hop has a carrot.

Ben tugs the carrot.

Hop tugs the carrot.

Ben and Sam tug it.

Hop and Flop tug it.

Ben and Sam and Dad tug it.

Tug! Tug!

Hop and Flop and Lop tug it.

Tug! Tug!

Pop!

They all have some carrot.

The Letter "S"

Trace the lowercase and uppercase letter with a finger. Sound out the letter.

Around, around

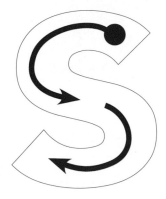

Around, around

Some words to familiarize:

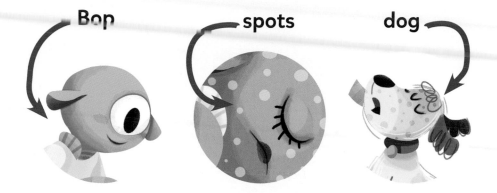

Bop   spots   dog

High-frequency words:

no   and   of

Tips for Reading *Lots of Spots*

- *Practice the words listed above before reading the story.*
- *If the reader struggles with any of the other words, ask them to look for sounds they know in the word. Encourage them to sound out the words and help them read the words if necessary.*
- *After reading the story, ask the reader why Bop's mom, dad, and dog had lots of spots.*

Fun Activity

Count all the spots in the story!

Lots of Spots

Bop's mom had lots of spots.

Bop's dad had lots of spots.

Bop's dog had lots of spots.

Bop had no spots.

Mom had no spots.

Dad had no spots.

Dog had no spots.

Bop had lots of spots!

EARLY BIRD
STORIES™

COLOR		GRL
Purple	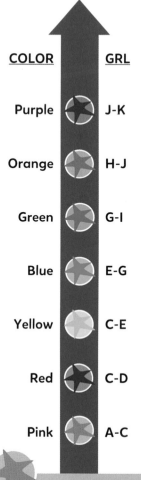	J-K
Orange		H-J
Green		G-I
Blue		E-G
Yellow		C-E
Red		C-D
Pink		A-C

Leveled for Guided Reading

Early Bird Stories have been edited and leveled by leading educational consultants to correspond with guided reading levels. The levels are assigned by taking into account the content, language style, layout, and phonics used in each book.